The Case of the
Best Pet Ever

Read all the Jigsaw Jones Mysteries

And Don't Miss . . .

Coming Soon . . .

The Case of the
Best Pet Ever

by James Preller
& Howie Dewin
illustrated by Jamie Smith
cover illustration by R. W. Alley

A
LITTLE APPLE
PAPERBACK

SCHOLASTIC INC.
New York Toronto London Auckland Sydney
Mexico City New Delhi Hong Kong Buenos Aires

For Seamus, my dog.

— JP

For Hap, the finest dog of my childhood.

— HD

No part of this work may be reproduced in whole or in part, or stored in a retrieval system, or transmitted in any form or by any means, electronic, mechanical, photocopying, recording, or otherwise, without written permission of the publisher. For information regarding permission, write to Scholastic Inc., Attention: Permissions Department, 557 Broadway, New York, NY 10012.

ISBN 0-439-55995-2

Text copyright © 2003 by James Preller. Illustrations copyright © 2003 by Scholastic Inc. All rights reserved. Published by Scholastic Inc. SCHOLASTIC, LITTLE APPLE, A JIGSAW JONES MYSTERY, and associated logos are trademarks and/or registered trademarks of Scholastic Inc.

12 11 10 9 8 7 6 5 4 3 2 1   3 4 5 6 7 8/0

Printed in the U.S.A.
First printing, October 2003

40

CONTENTS

Chapter One
Teddy

For the first six days of my life, I didn't have a name. I was the fifth and last kid born in my family. After Billy, Hillary, Nick, and Daniel, my parents couldn't decide on a name for little old me. For six days, I was known as "the baby."

I say this because my mom found a box of old baby pictures today while I was doing a jigsaw puzzle. She got all misty-eyed and blubbery, saying things like, "Goo-goo, ga-ga," and calling me baby

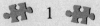 1

names. That is, after she finished yelling at my dog, Rags.

Mom says Rags is a shoe thief. But Ragsy just lies there, sprawled on the carpet. His eyes follow her but he doesn't lift his head. It's like he can't figure out what the fuss is about. I think it's kind of funny. But Mom is missing three different shoes and she doesn't think it's funny at all.

So anyway, for six days my parents called me "the baby" because they figured the right name would pop into their heads. By day four, the names that had popped into my dad's head were Carlos, Lars, Ferdinand, and Slippy.

Mom said, "No, No, NO!" and "Slippy?! Are you *trying* to make me crazy?!"

On day six, she said that I was as cute as a teddy bear. (Don't laugh.)

"Sure," my dad agreed. "A bald, pink, wrinkled teddy bear."

So they named me Teddy (even though

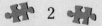 2

my official name is Theodore Andrew Jones). No one ever called me Teddy, though. And that's a good thing — since Teddy is a crummy name for a detective. A detective should be named Nick or Sam or Derek or Roscoe. You know, a cool, tough-sounding name.

Anyway, now I'm in second grade. And these days everybody calls me Jigsaw, except for my brothers, who usually call me Worm and Shorty.

I got the nickname because I love jigsaw puzzles. But the one thing I like more than doing jigsaw puzzles is solving mysteries. See, I'm a detective. And I've got the decoder ring to prove it.

I have a partner, too. Her name is Mila Yeh (sounds like "my-la yay!"). We've found missing hamsters, stolen baseball cards, and disappearing dinosaurs. We've had cases with spooky ghosts, marshmallow monsters, and walking scarecrows.

It's all right there on our business card: "For a dollar a day, we make problems go away."

It beats selling Kool-Aid for a living.

"You really did look like a teddy bear," Mom gushed.

Oh, brother.

Woof-woof, woof!

Thanks to Rags, I didn't have to answer. Rags is like a walking doorbell with fur and a cold wet tongue.

I figured Mila was at the door. There was a big case brewing and we needed to talk. Bobby Solofsky had called that afternoon. He said he wanted to hire us and he was coming over to explain.

It would take a lot of explaining.

You see, Solofsky has been a stone in my shoe since kindergarten. He's always bragging about how he's a better detective than I am. So why, I wondered, would he want to hire us?

There was definitely something fishy here — and it wasn't my tuna sandwich.

Chapter Two
Grand Prize Gone!

I can always tell when Mila's coming. Her singing enters the room five minutes before she does. Today she was singing "Where, Oh, Where Has My Little Dog Gone," only she changed the words around.

"Why, oh, why did Solofsky call?
What, oh, what could he want?"

I was glad to see her. This Solofsky thing was bugging me. We needed to talk before he showed up.

 7

Before Mila could say anything, I put my finger to my nose. That was our secret signal. Billy (my favorite brother) was sprawled on a living room chair, talking to his new girlfriend. Get this — her name is Rain. Not Snow, not Sleet, but Rain. She sounded like a drip to me.

We went to my tree house for privacy.

"Spill it," Mila said. "Why does Solofsky want to hire us?"

"No idea," I answered. "But I do know this. Bobby Solofsky can't be trusted. I don't want anything to do with this case."

Mila frowned, pulling on her long black hair. "This is business," she said. "It's not personal. We should hear what he's got to say."

I guess she was right.

Suddenly, Rags started barking. Solofsky was here. I downed a glass of grape juice and wiped my mouth.

Bobby Solofsky climbed the tree house ladder. His face was a scowl. I waited for him to speak. But he just sat there. The minutes crawled by like sick cockroaches.

"So?" I said.

"So?" he replied.

Mila started to hum. She couldn't help herself. "A needle pulling thread," she sang.

I ignored her.

"Time is money, Solofsky," I said. "What's up?"

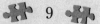

He grunted and shrugged. Then he ran his tongue across the front of his teeth and made a gross sucking sound. I've known camels with better manners.

"First off," Solofsky began, "I'd solve this case myself, but I'm not allowed at the scene of the crime."

I scratched the back of my neck and listened.

"Start from the beginning," Mila urged. "Tell us everything you remember."

I opened my detective journal.

"I have to clear my good name," Solofsky said angrily. "That guy in the store blamed me for no reason. I put the medal back exactly where I found it!"

"Slow down," I told Solofsky. "What guy? What store? What medal?"

I poured him a glass of grape juice. That seemed to calm him down. "Here's the deal," Solofsky said. "One, I was in that new pet store last Saturday. Two, the grand

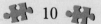

prize for their animal talent show was on the counter. I picked it up. Then I put it right back down. Now the owner says I stole it."

"What did he say, exactly?" I prodded.

Solofsky groaned. "He said, 'You should return the medal before your karma turns colors.'"

"Your car turns . . . what?" I repeated.

"I told you he was weird," Bobby answered. He wagged a finger in a circular motion beside his ear. "The guy is cuckoo for Cocoa Puffs. He's bonkers. He's a Froot Loop, I tell ya. And I've been framed!"

"Tell us more about this pet shop," Mila said.

"It's crazy," Solofsky scoffed. "There's this really loud-talking parrot. And different animals run around free. Like, um, there's a cat and a ferret."

I glanced down at my notes. "Let me get this straight, Solofsky. You're not allowed

in the store because the owner thinks you stole some kind of medal. Is that right?"

Solofsky nodded.

"And you want to hire us to help clear your name?"

"That's right," Solofsky said.

"When is the contest?" Mila asked. "And is this medal the grand prize?"

"I was getting to that," Solofsky snorted. "It's an animal talent show. The contest is this Saturday. The winner gets this cool gold medal. I figure it's worth a few bucks, for sure," he added.

I looked Solofsky in the eye. "I've got to ask," I said. "Did you take it?"

"No way," he blurted.

I nodded. "One more thing," I said. "Why do you care if you're not allowed in the store? You don't even have a pet."

Bobby tapped his foot. His eyes narrowed. "There is this little white puppy," he confessed. "She's kind of cute and I like

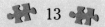 13

to visit her. You know, play with her and stuff."

I'll admit it. That surprised me. I never figured Solofsky for the cute puppy type.

A scream came from my house. It was my mom again. "Rags!" she hollered.

Another shoe was missing.

Yeesh.

I locked eyes with Mila. Then I pushed a glass jar toward Solofsky. "We'll look into it for you," I promised. "Three dollars ought to be enough to get us started."

"Three dollars?!" Solofsky protested.

I shrugged. "That's the price, pal. Hire us, or don't hire us. It makes no difference to me."

Solofsky grumbled, muttered, and moaned. Then he shoved three crumpled dollars in the jar.

Chapter Three

Fur, Fins & Feathers

It was time to take a little trip to the pet store. My brother Billy was happy to drive Mila and me. We brought Rags along for the ride. Billy never missed a chance to borrow my mom's car. Besides, he told me, his girlfriend worked there.

"Rain?" I asked.

He nodded.

"What kind of name is that?" Mila asked.

"Her parents are a little . . . different," Billy explained.

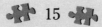

"No kidding," I answered. "Does she have a sister named Partly Cloudy?"

"Har-har, detective," Billy groaned. He pulled up the car in front of the store.

"Come on, Ragsy," I said. "We've got a little detective work to do."

It was good for Ragsy to get out of the house. He'd been making my mom a little crazy lately. I figured the pet store owner might give me some advice on how to solve Ragsy's shoe problem. It was the perfect cover. No one would suspect Mila and I were really snooping around for clues.

There was a sign over the door.

FUR, FINS & FEATHERS

I pulled off my baseball cap and scratched my head. "Kind of a weird name," I murmured to Mila as we stepped inside.

"Hi, Billy!" A tall girl with white teeth and

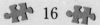

twinkling eyes waved to my brother from behind the counter.

"Who-o-o-oa!" a shaggy-haired man exclaimed. "My daughter and I were just talking about you, Billy, and like, wow, here you are!" He snapped his fingers in astonishment. As if Billy walking in the door was the most amazing thing that had ever happened.

Go figure.

"Hey, Jax," Billy said, squeezing my shoulder. "This is my little brother Jigsaw. He's looking for some advice."

Okay, confession time: I wasn't exactly honest with Billy about the case. After all, his girlfriend was a suspect. That's the thing in my line of work. Everybody's a suspect, and anything is possible. It can put a detective in a tight spot. I didn't want Billy to know that I was checking out a robbery — and that his own girlfriend might be the thief. After all, she was at the scene of the crime.

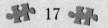 17

"Far-out," Jax said. "Where are my glasses?" He patted his pockets, scratched his head, and looked around the store. "The animal kingdom is full of sticky-fingered critters," he mumbled. "I love it! Where's my green tea?"

Mila rolled her eyes. Neither of us had a clue about what Jax had just said. Mila nodded at a sign on the counter.

"Wow," I said, pointing to the sign. "You're having a talent show?"

Rain drew her lips together in a tight frown. "Yes, but," she said, "the grand prize is missing. My father thinks a boy took it this weekend."

"Were there witnesses?" I asked.

"Not exactly," Rain said. "I saw the boy holding the prize. And the next minute, it was gone."

"What will you do without a prize?" Mila asked. She poked me with her elbow and crept off to look around the store.

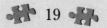 19

"We'll think of something," Rain said.

I tried to keep Rain talking while Mila checked out the store.

"Maybe I can solve the mystery for you," I offered.

I pulled out my detective journal. "Give me the facts," I said.

Rain smiled at me. "Well, okay. Why not? There was an older couple looking at the fish. And there was a girl named Danika who was upset about the animals in cages. . . ."

"*Animals in cages! Animals in cages!*" a high-pitched voice squawked. I turned and saw a parrot pacing on a stand, screaming its head off. "*Cages! Cages!*" it repeated over and over.

Suddenly, a cat and a ferret raced over my shoes, through my legs, and across the floor.

"Sorry." Rain laughed. "The cat's name is Rainbow, and this is Curiosity, our ferret. They're both free to roam around the store." Rain picked up the ferret and gently

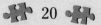

stroked its head. The ferret reached up and playfully batted at Rain's earring.

Meanwhile, Rags was pretty much flipping out. He whined and strained on his leash. "*Shhh*, Ragsy," I said. "It's okay."

Mila pointed to a photograph on the wall of Rain and her family. She called me over. "Look at this, Jigsaw," Mila said with a laugh. "The ferret is sitting on that lady's head!"

Solofsky was right about one thing. This

sure was a nutty little store. "That Jax," I whispered. "He's a little . . ."

"Weird?" Mila suggested.

"Yeah," I agreed. "And nobody actually saw Bobby take the prize. As strange as this might seem, Solofsky might be telling the truth."

Woof, woof! Rags pawed at me in alarm. The ferret, Curiosity, was trying to tackle his tail.

Jax quickly came over. "It's cool, mini-dude," he cooed calmly. "Ferrets are lively little critters," he explained. "They're always into something or other. But they sure make life interesting!"

It was time to go. Between the squawking and the meowing and the barking, I'd had enough of the wonders of nature for one day. I wanted some peace and quiet so I could think. At Jax's suggestion, I bought a cheap chew toy for Ragsy. Maybe this would keep him from stealing Mom's shoes.

Chapter Four
Behave!

Guess who wasn't talking about the animal talent show at school the next day?

Nobody!

And I was getting worried. If I didn't find the missing prize, Solofsky would tell everyone that I couldn't crack the case. I wondered if Solofsky was setting me up. This could all be another one of his tricks to make me look bad.

Before the morning bell, kids were lying on the reading rug, talking at desks, or just hanging around. By the cubbies, I heard

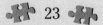 23

Lucy Hiller tell Mila that she was planning to enter the contest. "But before I finished filling out the form in the store, I noticed my glitter purse was missing." Lucy complained, "I still don't know what happened to it."

Hmmm. That made for two robberies at Fur, Fins & Feathers. I wondered if the person who took the grand prize also stole Lucy's purse.

Joey Pignattano walked in the door. He looked like he'd just lost a fight with a sticker bush. He had scratches all over his hands and face.

"What happened to you?" I asked.

"Four words, Jigsaw," Joey said, glumly holding up four fingers. "Never dress a cat."

"Eyes are —" Ms. Gleason stood at her desk and waited for us to answer her.

"WATCHING!" some of us answered.

"Ears are —"

"LISTENING!" more of us answered.

We moved to our desks. I bumped into Danika Starling. She was a suspect, too. I'd have to get some answers from her sooner or later.

"Hands are —"

"QUIET!" everyone answered.

"Feet are —"

"STILL!" we answered loudly.

"Lips are —"

"SMILING!" we shouted. Everyone was seated and paying attention.

Ms. Gleason smiled. "I know everyone is excited about the animal talent show," she said. "So as part of our study on animal behavior, I'm offering extra credit if you go to the contest and write a short report."

Everybody started chattering again.

"Are you going to enter your basset hound?" Nicole Rodriguez asked Ms. Gleason.

"Oh, goodness no!" Ms. Gleason said

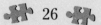 26

with a laugh. "Brutus doesn't do tricks. But he does have some interesting behaviors. Like the way he cleans himself, eats, plays, and finds a safe sleeping place. In fact, all animals have their own way of doing things.

"Which brings us to our next assignment. I want each of you to choose an animal and list four interesting ways in which that animal behaves. Use your own pet if you have one."

Oh, great, I thought. Rags in action. He sleeps. He drools. He sleeps some more. I scribbled a quick picture.

"I saw some really cool snakes at the zoo on Saturday," Eddie Becker blurted out. "Can I use them?"

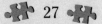

"Yes, you may choose any animal you like," Ms. Gleason answered. "Even our class hamster!"

Just before recess, I got a secret message from Mila.

MT M T TH TR SWNG. HV NWS.

"So, what's up?" I asked Mila on the playground. I held up her coded message and read, "Meet me at the tire swing. I have news." It was one of our favorite codes. Mila had left out all the vowels!

"Rain was right," Mila said. "Danika was in the pet store at the time of the robbery. She was protesting the treatment of the animals."

"Huh?"

"Danika thinks some of the cages are too small," Mila explained.

My list of suspects was growing. Danika

Starling is room 201's biggest animal lover. I wondered if she was mad enough at the pet store to steal.

"I've got an idea," Mila said. "You should enter Rags in the contest."

"Rags? In a *talent* show?" I laughed. "Rags is a good dog, but he doesn't exactly have any talents."

"It will get you behind the scenes," Mila urged. "It might help us break the case."

"Yeah," I muttered. "And I'll get laughed at when Rags sleeps through the whole thing!"

Chapter Five
The Case of the Missing Talent

"Little Holmes!" Jax shouted in greeting when I walked in the store after school.

"Hi, Jigsaw," Rain said. "I was just telling Dad that you're a detective. Are you here to try to solve the mystery?"

"Actually, my mom is parked outside. I just want to enter Rags in the contest."

"Awesome, Little Holmes!" Jax shouted again.

"Dad loves Sherlock Holmes," Rain explained.

I nodded politely and tried to put a smile on my face. Little Holmes? *Yuck*. Theodore was bad enough. I didn't need another name. "You can call me Jigsaw," I suggested.

Jax was a suspect. By pretending that the grand prize was stolen, he wouldn't have to spend money on a giveaway. It was definitely a motive. The oldest one in the world, in fact. Money.

I went over the list of suspects in my mind. Danika told Mila that she had changed her mind about the store. Now she thought it was really cool that some of the animals were allowed to run around free. It didn't seem likely that Danika was the thief. And Rain said the older couple never even came to the front counter. So they couldn't have done it.

That left three suspects: Solofsky, Jax, and Rain. But Rain seemed too nice to be a thief. Still, I needed proof. Hard facts. Right

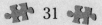 31

now, it was like trying to do a puzzle with some of the pieces missing.

"What talent does your dog have?" Rain asked.

"That's the problem," I grumbled. "He doesn't seem to have one."

Rain pinched her lower lip thoughtfully. "All animals have talent. You could give Rags a doggie IQ test," she suggested.

"Brilliant idea!" Jax cheered. He fished around the cluttered counter until he found a magazine article. He handed it to me. The headline read: HOW SMART IS YOUR DOG?

"Thanks," I said, shoving the magazine into my backpack.

Squawk! "Funny ferret! Funny ferret!"

I nearly jumped out of my socks in surprise. Rainbow and Curiosity, the cat and the ferret, darted across the floor. *Clang, ka-boom!* They knocked over a display of cat toys. At least Rags wasn't this much

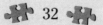

trouble. Sleeping and drooling didn't cause headaches.

Rain looked at me and laughed. "It's just the animals."

Squawk. *"Just the animals! Just the animals!"* echoed the parrot.

Rain excused herself to see to another customer. That's when I got a crazy idea. I walked up to Polly the parrot. "Okay, my feathered friend," I whispered to Polly. "It

looks like you're my only witness. Tell me. Do you think Rain took the prize?"

Squawk. "Rain took the prize! Rain took the prize!"

"Good work, Little Holmes!" Jax shouted happily. "You've solved the mystery! Far-out!"

"Very funny, Dad," Rain said. "Polly only repeats what she hears!"

I laughed it off, too. Very funny. Ha-ha. But deep down inside, I had a feeling that Polly was trying to tell me something.

"Hey, Dad," Rain asked Jax, "have you seen my sparkly hair clip? I'm sure I left it here on the counter."

I suddenly noticed Solofsky staring inside the store, his nose smushed against the front window. He looked sad and lonely and more than a little like a piggy. After I filled in the contest entry form, I went outside to talk to him.

"How's Bubbles?" he asked me.

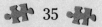 35

"Bubbles?"

"The white puppy," he said. "Does she seem happy?"

"Sure, Solofsky," I said. "I guess so. I mean, about as happy as a puppy in a pet store can be. But between us, I think Bubbles needs a boy."

Solofsky's face brightened. "You do?"

"Every puppy needs a kid," I said. "Don't you know that?"

I headed toward my mom's car. Rain's sparkly hair clip was missing. And Bobby Solofsky hadn't even been in the store.

Very interesting.

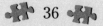

Chapter Six

IQ Test

Rain and Billy showed up at my house like two little lovebirds, arm in arm.

Yuck.

"You're just in time for the doggie IQ test," I told them.

Mila read aloud from the magazine. "It says here that the best way to measure your dog's IQ is to test his problem-solving skills. It also says that smart dogs obey well."

"Sit!" I commanded Rags. Einstein wagged his tail and barked.

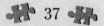

"Well, he's awake," Billy noted cheerfully. Rain giggled.

"Hey, Rain," I asked. "I was wondering. Do you know what the missing grand prize was worth?"

Billy eyed me closely.

"I sure do," Rain answered. "Dad told me it cost forty-five dollars."

Sometimes a detective has to stir things up just to see how they fall. Half smiling, I asked Rain: "You didn't take the grand prize for yourself, did you?"

Billy gave me a funny look. "What are you asking, Jigsaw?"

Rain smiled. "It's okay, Billy. Jigsaw is a detective. He has to look at all the possible suspects."

I could see why Billy liked her.

"Believe me, Jigsaw," Rain said. "I'm not happy about this missing prize, either. After all, the talent show was my idea."

Mila twirled her hair. I could tell we were

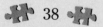

thinking the same thing. Rain wouldn't ruin her own talent show. And come to think of it, Rain wouldn't take her own hair clip, either.

Mila spoke up. "Back to the IQ test! First, put a towel over Rags's head. We have to time how long it takes for him to shake it off."

Fifteen minutes later, Rags was asleep under the towel. It was pretty clear he had flunked the test. Billy and Rain got bored and went outside. Mila had to go home for a piano lesson. I sat alone, staring unhappily at my sleeping dog.

I had to come up with a new trick for Rags. I decided to teach him to steal a shoe on command. All he had to do was pick up a shoe and drop it in a box. It wasn't the greatest trick in the world, but it was better than nothing.

I pulled the towel off his head. That only made Rags snore louder.

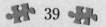

Later that night, after a long bath, I called Mila on the phone. "Tomorrow, we've got a secret mission," I whispered.

"Yeah, what's that?" Mila asked.

I took a deep breath. "I have to search Solofsky's room. And I can't do it without your help."

"But I thought you didn't think Solofsky took the medal," Mila replied.

"I didn't," I said, "and I don't. But we need to make sure. Are you willing to help me?"

Chapter Seven

Dropping Clues

I'd never seen Solofsky so down and out. All day in school, he just slumped in his chair and sighed. When he answered the door at his house, he looked about as happy as a cat in a car wash.

"Hi, Solofsky," I said.

"Hi," he groaned.

"We came over to review the case," I told him.

He nodded.

"The contest is two days away," Mila said. "And all we've found are dead ends."

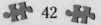 42

"Is there somewhere private we can go?" I asked. "Your bedroom, maybe?"

Thankfully, Solofsky had no problem with that idea. Once we were inside his room, it was just a matter of getting a good look around.

Solofsky's room was a disaster area.

He frowned. "My dad says I have to clean my room or he's going to explode."

"It looks like there's already been an explosion," Mila commented. She picked up a few toys from the floor.

Solofsky picked up a Lego rocket ship and carelessly set it on a shelf. It dropped to the floor with a crash, breaking into pieces.

Solofsky just sighed.

He slumped on the bed, his head in his heads. "Sorry, guys. Maybe you should go. I don't feel like doing anything."

"No!" Mila exclaimed. She gave me a worried look. "I mean, oh, no . . . you don't.

 43

We'll help you clean up your room. That always makes me happy!"

"It does?" I asked.

Mila gave me a sharp poke in the ribs. "Yes, *detective*, it does," she insisted.

"Right, right!" I agreed. I understood the plan. By cleaning up, we could search Solofsky's room and he wouldn't suspect a thing.

I picked up a smelly sock. *Phew.*

"I'll straighten up your desk," Mila

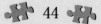

offered. She opened drawers and shuffled papers.

I cleared my throat. "Hey, Solofsky. You got any grape juice in the house?"

"I could make some Kool-Aid," he offered.

"That'd be great," I said, clapping him on the back. "You go do that while Mila and I search, er, I mean, *clean* your room."

Mila and I went through all of Solofsky's things slowly, carefully. I patted down the clothes in his closet. I searched likely hiding places — under his mattress, inside his shoes, on top of high shelves.

All I found was a stale bag of Doritos and a flat can of ginger ale. No grand prize anywhere.

When Bobby came back to the room, he seemed to be in a better mood. "I heard other stuff was missing from the store," he said. "Doesn't that clear me of the crime?"

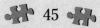 45

"Not exactly," I said. "You won't be in the clear until we find the real thief."

"Or thieves," Mila said.

"Thieves?" Solofsky wondered.

"It could be more than one person," I said. "Anything is possible."

Solofsky sighed. He gathered up the comic books and carelessly threw them on his bedside table. They toppled over onto the carpet.

He suddenly turned and looked at us with desperate eyes. "You've gotta help me," he pleaded. "I've got to be allowed back in that store. Jigsaw, Mila — you're my last hope."

Chapter Eight
Tricky Business

Before class started on Friday morning, I sat down at my desk to read through my detective journal. But it was hard to think. Everyone was talking about the talent show.

Kim Lewis was training a jumping frog. Nicole Rodriguez had a cat that could do back flips. Joey had, thankfully, given up the idea of dressing his cat. Instead, he was trying to train a worm to roll over. Go figure. Helen Zuckerman wouldn't stop talking about her poodle. She claimed it spoke French.

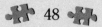

I closed my notebook and got out my animal behavior folder. I'd been so busy with the case that I hadn't done the homework. I started a list:

Rags
1. He sleeps.
2. He drools.
3. He barks at the doorbell.

I tapped my eraser and tried to think of a good number four. I thought about what we do when Rags and I are together. The truth is, Rags doesn't do much. But somehow, he's good company anyway. I started to write "good company," but I erased it. It wasn't really a behavior.

Then I thought about our training sessions. Rags had learned to pick up the shoe on command, but he always missed the box when he set it down. I added to my list:

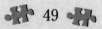

4. He never gets things where he means to put them.

That was it! I suddenly realized Bobby and Rags had something in common.

I scribbled a coded message and passed it to Mila:

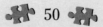

W MST G T TH STR FTR SCHL. THNK
KNW WHR TH PRZ S!

She read it, smiled, and rubbed a finger across her nose. "We must go to the store after school. I think I know where the prize is!" She got the message!

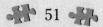

Chapter nine
The Hiding Place

I had the answer and it didn't get anyone in trouble! The thief wasn't Rain or Jax or Bobby. At least, not really Bobby. Not on purpose, anyway.

"Hi, Jax!" I called out as Mila and I walked into the store on Friday afternoon.

"Mila! Little Holmes! What gives?" Jax greeted us.

"Jigsaw thinks he may have solved the case," Mila said proudly.

"Far-out!" Jax exclaimed.

I got down on my hands and knees and

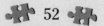

searched the floor. I was sure Bobby had meant to put the prize back on the counter, but missed. I'd seen him do the same thing when putting stuff away in his room. He was careless with the Legos, and they fell. Same thing with the comic books. Bobby is just like Rags! *They never get things where they mean to put them!*

I was sure that the prize had fallen to the floor and got kicked under the counter. But I was wrong. There was nothing there but

some dust bunnies. It hadn't even been swept out lately.

"Rats!" I muttered.

"Last cage on the left," Jax said.

"No," I said. "I mean *rats*! I was wrong. Rats!"

"Rats! Rats!" the parrot squawked.

A woman at the counter looked startled.

"It's cool, ma'am," Jax reassured her. "No rats on the loose. Just a talking parrot!"

Suddenly, Rainbow and Curiosity made one of their mad dashes through the store. Curiosity stopped, spun, and began to nibble on the silver buckle of the woman's shoe.

Naturally, the woman screamed.

The parrot kept squawking, *"Rats! Rats!"*

The woman, looking flustered, patted her pockets. "My keys," she said, looking around the store in alarm. "I don't seem to have my keys!"

She looked as puzzled as I felt.

* * *

That night, I was as frustrated as a dentist in a candy store. I still had no answers for the case. There was a robber in that pet store, all right. But I couldn't figure out who it was.

I decided to work on the trick with Rags. I gave him a shoe and pointed to the box.

"Rags!" I yelled. "Don't just drop it on the floor!"

My dad stuck his head in from the kitchen. "Having a tough time with old Ragsy?"

"He's hopeless!" I complained. "What a useless dog!"

Right away, I felt bad for saying it.

Even Rags seemed to understand. He looked at me with hurt eyes.

"I guess you haven't been able to teach that old dog a new trick," my father said. He gave Rags a friendly pat.

"No, I haven't," I growled.

55

"Well, don't give up on Ragsy. He'll learn. It just may take some time. Besides, Rags thinks you're about the greatest person on the planet. Look how he watches you, Jigsaw," Dad said.

I looked at Rags. And he looked at me. And I remembered all the good times we had together. Squirting him with a hose. Pretending he was a turkey and chasing him around the yard on Thanksgiving. Sleeping together in my bed, snug and warm.

That's what he did best of all, I realized. The big fur ball loved me with all his heart. Every minute of every hour of every day.

And that's no small trick.

My father patted me on the shoulder. "A wise man once said, 'Try to be the person your dog thinks you are.'"

He smiled and headed back into the kitchen. "I have an important meeting with

a cheesecake," he explained. Rags followed him. Rags liked cheesecake, too.

Later that night, after I finished my spelling homework, I grabbed a plastic bag. It was time to walk Rags. But I could only find one of my sneakers.

"Rags," I muttered to myself. "Now he's going after *my* shoes."

I wanted to catch him in the act. I looked high. I looked low. No Rags. I tried the basement. Nothing. When I started back upstairs I heard a noise. I pushed open the door to the furnace room.

That's where I saw Ragsy's tail, poking out from behind the furnace. "Hey, boy," I called sweetly.

Rags popped his head out. My Nike was in his mouth, covered with drool.

"Gross!" I said. I climbed behind the furnace to grab the shoe.

That's when I saw it: Ragsy's stash. Four

of Mom's missing shoes — and about
seventeen socks that I didn't even know
were missing. They were all shoved in a
dark corner behind the furnace.

Ragsy's treasure.

Chapter Ten

Suspects by the Dozen!

I realized that Ragsy's hiding place was the missing piece of the puzzle. Faster than a dog can steal a shoe, it was clear that I had missed dozens of possible suspects. They were all at the scene of the crime — and they were still there!

It was Saturday. The day of the contest. I called Mila and told her to meet me at the store. When Rags and I got there, the store was already crowded. Animals were barking and screeching and hissing. Rain was putting the finishing touches on the stage in front of the counter. Folding chairs were set up all the way to the door. The place was a zoo!

"What's up?" Mila said when she saw me. *Woof! Woof!*

I held tight to Ragsy's leash.

"Rags helped me solve the case!" I said. I told her what I had discovered. "He can't be the only animal in the world that likes to hide things."

"But which animal is it?" Mila asked. "There must be dozens of suspects in the store."

Then she snapped her fingers. Mila ran to the photograph on the wall. "Remember Rain's hair clip?" she exclaimed. "I bet that ferret was going after the clip in this woman's hair!"

Sure enough, Mila was right. In the photo with the ferret atop the woman's head, we could see part of a clip in the ferret's paws.

"Jax did say ferrets were always getting

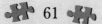

into trouble," I remembered. "But we weren't paying attention."

"Now for the hard part," Mila said. "We have to find the ferret's hiding place!"

Woof!

Rags and I headed to the back of the store. Mila took the front. Rags was panting and pulling on his leash. More kids were

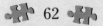

showing up. The show was minutes away and the ferret was nowhere to be seen.

Mila shook her head as we met at the stage. "I asked Jax to help us," she said. "But Curiosity isn't in any of his usual places."

The seats were filling up. Ms. Gleason waved at me. Danika was talking to Jax. It

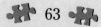

seemed like everyone from room 201 was in the store.

"Any luck?" Rain asked me hopefully.

I frowned.

"That's okay," she said with a smile. "You tried. And the show must go on. You and Rags are last. Right after Wingnut O'Brien's hamster act."

My stomach flipped and my knees flopped. Rags and I were about to go down in history as the worst pet trick ever. Mila found a seat. She held onto Rags while I searched the supply closet.

"Welcome to the First Annual Fur, Fins & Feathers Talent Show!" Rain announced. Everybody cheered. I stood in the dark closet and tried to think like a ferret.

It wasn't easy.

I looked behind the bags of dog food. In the distance, I heard Helen's poodle bark in French — *Oui! Oui! Oui!*

Lucy Hiller went, then Joey with his

crazy worm trick. One by one, I heard contestants show off their pets as the crowd cheered. I looked behind every bag, box, and can. No ferret.

"Wingnut O'Brien and his hamster, Hermie!" I heard Rain announce.

Rags and I were next. He had never once done his trick and the grand prize was still missing. I felt like a failure.

I headed back to Mila and Rags. Wingnut was singing a duet with Hermie. The hamster squeaked along to "Mary Had a Little Lamb." The crowd roared with laughter.

Just great, I thought. Rags and I have to follow the best act in the show.

Chapter Eleven
Rags to Riches

Squawk! Squawk! Squawk!

Polly the parrot was screeching at the top of her lungs. The cat and ferret tore through the crowd, climbing up on seats, diving, leaping, scrambling in and over everything in sight.

My heart leaped. Curiosity had something in its mouth.

"Hey!" Ms. Gleason cried. "That ferret stole my earring!"

Mila raced up to me. "The parrot is like an alarm system," she exclaimed. "When

the ferret steals something, the parrot squawks!"

We took off after the ferret with Rags leading the way. We followed them down the dog toys aisle and around a corner. But then Rags barked and Mila and I stopped short. Curiosity had vanished.

Rain tried to calm down the crowd.

"Out of control, Little Holmes!" Jax called out. "Where'd the little critter go?"

"Thin air," I muttered.

That's when Rags did the most amazing thing. He sniffed the floor, stood on his hind legs, and barked at some dog beds on a shelf.

Loudly.

Over and over again.

"Crazy dog!" Jax said gleefully. He reached his arm up and the ferret jumped onto his shoulder. Jax smiled and pulled down a big stuffed dog bed.

There on the bed lay a bunch of shiny

objects, including Rain's hair clip, a set of keys, a shiny purse, an earring, and the grand-prize medal!

Jax held up the prize. "Rock on, Little Holmes! You solved the mystery!"

Rain clapped her hands together. Ms. Gleason gave me a thumbs-up. And Rags barked and drooled and rested his bones on the cool tile floor.

I glanced toward the front window. Sure enough, there was Solofsky, nose pressed against the glass.

Jax saw Solofsky, too. "Excuse me," Jax said. "I have an apology to make."

Rain gave me a big hug. "You're a hero, Jigsaw!" she exclaimed.

Nope, I thought. Rags was the real hero. It seemed wrong to ask him to do a silly shoe trick after such great doggy detective work. But people were pushing us toward the stage and cheering.

Rain set out a box and an old shoe. Mila

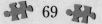

gave me a push toward the stage. Rags and I were about to go from hero to ha-ha!

I looked Rags in the eye. He looked back at me like he thought I was the best person on the planet. I wasn't, but I didn't tell Rags that. I heard Dad's voice in my head. *Try to be the person your dog thinks you are.* So I took a deep breath, looked at Rags with all the love in my heart, and said, "Steal the shoe, Ragsy."

Rags picked up the shoe in his mouth. He

walked across the stage. He looked at me once, then dropped the shoe into the box.

As if he'd done it a thousand times.

The crowd exploded.

I couldn't believe it.

My old dog had learned a new trick!

In the end, Wingnut and his hamster won the contest. That was okay. Everybody knew Rags was the best pet ever.

"I should have figured it out," Rain said. "Ferrets are known for their sneaky behavior. Hiding things is not a surprise."

I saw Jax talking with Bobby. Jax was leaning close to him, speaking softly, shaking his hand. Bobby had a huge grin on his face. He raced over to Bubbles and they tumbled on the floor together.

"Guess you're off the hook," I said to Bobby.

"Not only that," Bobby bragged. "I just got a job as a dog walker."

I waited for him to thank me. But he didn't. Solofsky just played with his puppy. Happy as can be.

"You're welcome," I finally said.

"Oh, right," Bobby replied. "Thanks, Jigsaw. Too bad it took you so long, but I guess you tried pretty hard."

Yeesh.

Zebras never change their stripes. And Solofsky will always be a stone in my shoe.

But none of it mattered. The case was solved. Rags thought I was the best person in the world. And I felt the same way about him.